Take Care of You

Dona Herweck Rice

Publishing Credits

Rachelle Cracchiolo, M.S.Ed., *Publisher*
Conni Medina, M.A.Ed., *Managing Editor*
Nika Fabienke, Ed.D., *Content Director*
Véronique Bos, *Creative Director*
Shaun N. Bernadou, *Art Director*
Carol Huey-Gatewood, M.A.Ed., *Editor*
John Leach, *Assistant Editor*
Courtney Roberson, *Senior Graphic Designer*

Image Credits: All images from iStock and/or Shutterstock.

Library of Congress Cataloging-in-Publication Data

Names: Rice, Dona, author.
Title: Take care of you / Dona Herweck Rice.
Description: Huntington Beach, CA : Teacher Created Materials, [2019] | Identifiers: LCCN 2018029741 (print) | LCCN 2018033699 (ebook) | ISBN 9781493899364 | ISBN 9781493898626
Subjects: LCSH: Readers (Primary)
Classification: LCC PE1119 (ebook) | LCC PE1119 .R468 2019 (print) | DDC 428.6/2--dc23
LC record available at https://lccn.loc.gov/2018029741

Teacher Created Materials
5301 Oceanus Drive
Huntington Beach, CA 92649-1030
www.tcmpub.com

ISBN 978-1-4938-9862-6

I0895251

You can 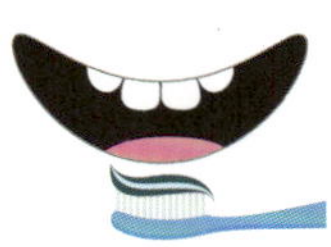 and 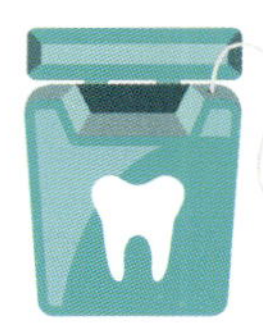

brush floss

some time each day.

You can  wash and  dry

some time each day.

You can  and 

eat drink

some time each day.

You can  and 

read write

some time each day.

You can  and 

run jump

some time each day.

You can  stand and  bend

some time each day.

You can  and 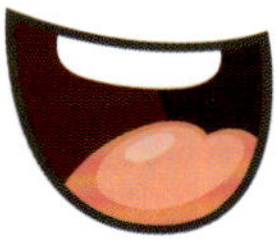

smile talk

some time each day.

You can  sit and  think

some time each day.

You can  and 

bathe hug

some time each day.

You can  and 

sleep dream

some time each day.

High-Frequency Words

New Words

can
day
each
some
time

Review Words

and
you